The Publisher's Acronym

Ray Clift lives in Adelaide with his wife Ann, who is an avid reader and a great cook. Between them they have several grandchildren. He writes, walks and sometimes talks to God. He uses his gym machine a few times each week. He plants native trees and feeds native birds. His 47 years in law enforcement has filled his head with many scenarios. Amongst those decades were 15 years as a court sheriff in Elizabeth. He managed to squeeze in another 15 years with the Reserve forces in Army Intelligence and the Military Police. Retirement saw him with a writers' group, which enabled 16 novellas which have been published with Ginninderra Press. His books are available in print and ebook editions from Amazon and other online sellers. He can be contacted through the Ginninderra Press website.

Also by Ray Clift and published by Ginninderra Press

Fiction

The Journey of Hamlyn Baylis Wells

Always In Denial

Smithy's Cupboard

Shaken & Stirred

Shalom Samuel

The Last Journey of Hamlin Baylis Wells

She Walks the Line

The Journeys of Hamlin Baylis Wells

Smithy & Suzie

Three in One

The Publisher

Non-fiction

Maybe Blue Ghosts

It's a Fine Line

Cops, Crooks, Courts & Spooks

Ray Clift

The Publisher's Acronym

Thanks to
my family
Sharon Kernot
Gary MacRae
Stephen and Brenda Matthews of Ginninderra Press

The Publisher's Acronym
ISBN 978 1 76041 355 2
Copyright text © Ray Clift 2017
Cover photos: judge's books – Anneke; fig jam – lenkaprusova

First published 2017 by
GINNINDERRA PRESS
PO Box 3461 Port Adelaide SA 5015
www.ginninderrapress.com.au

1

I loved her. Our bond was close, like two spoons almost welded together. I was a mess when she met me. She was the first and the only one who dared reach down into me. She coaxed and eased me up and out of my solitary hole. It took time, but she persisted and finally managed it. Then she set about straightening me out of my dowager hump, a posture which came from years of editing into the endless nights.

She spotted something in me that no other had. Just the way she looked at me. I recall the testimony of her eyes in my favour, the first time she let those eyes open for me. The time when they unveiled, warm into my face with those violet orbs.

I remember other things about her too: her hair, how it was combed over and brushed. She looked at me in those first days and she didn't have to say 'Believe me' like most people have to. She just had to look at me and I knew she believed in my worth, whether others did or not, and that she loved whether I did or not, and she was mine forever. No questions asked.

Nothing lasts forever – don't I know it. I lost her to a drunken, drugged semi-trailer driver on a straight road. One of those truckies who are all too frequently seen on the nightly news. One of those drivers who are stuck with tight schedules.

I lost interest in reading crap from then on until my son Joe rescued me from my time of the black dog. He encouraged me to seek counselling. He kept a weather eye on me. Others took over with the terrible rituals of the funeral – later on, ashes, which still remind me of her. She believed strongly in an afterlife. I wish she could talk to me from beyond.

2

My GP recommended treatment for my slide. Some pills, potions and creams were first on the list. Most of them caused some other problems, so other aids were prescribed. I contacted the firm who were to treat me. A cursory attendance came about and involved a lot more paperwork. As I was a veteran from way back, a naval chaplain was to sit in. I was not sure that I needed a hand to hold but those were the rules so I went along with it. I was ushered into the rooms and noted lots of paintings of flowers, sun and trees adorning the walls. Some were old French, some Constable and others modern art, which has never grabbed me.

I filled in the paperwork but was not of the mind that I ought to blurt out what was the germ of my troubles. Let them work it out. I had read numerous books on the subject before the visit and had a layman's point of view.

My depression paralleled my increasing weakness and inability to function as a man and a father and also as a publisher. I felt that a chance of additional treatment would not cheer me up. I was right. In my prior readings, many patients had struggled to separate themselves from their lives. They became sad having to struggle for life when they were prepared to die. This discrepancy between patients' readiness to die and the expectations of those around them caused the greatest grief and turmoil in patients. If the members of the helping profession were onto that problem, they could share patients' thoughts with the families. So there I am again self-medicating, with Doctor Google.

The first interview began with me asking, 'Do I have to talk very loudly?'

'No,' answered the doctor. 'That's all right. If we can't hear you, then we'll say so. Speak as loud as you like as long as you're comfortable.'

'The reason is that I'm physically very tired and dizzy,' I said.

There was lull while the doctor made some notes.

I spoke again. 'I find that it's too hard to feel physically up to par, even though I'm not really there. Sometimes I feel good, you know, like if I have good news or something like that. But that doesn't last for long.'

'What you're saying is we should talk about good things and not bad things,' said the doctor.

'Are we talking about good things?' was my comment.

'Is that what you're saying?' asked the doctor in turn.

'Oh no, not at all.'

The chaplain butted in. 'I think he's indicating that he wants a little moral support.'

'What I mean is if I sit here for about five minutes, I'm likely to collapse because I'm so bloody tired and I've been up so little of late. The tablets, I imagine.'

'So why don't we get right into the matter that we want to talk about?' said the doctor.

'Fine.'

'Your notes are blank pages. What's your work and your marital status?'

'I'm a book publisher, have been for years, and my beloved wife was killed in a car crash. How's that?'

'Was the crash recent?'

'That's how it seems to me.'

'When you're up to talking about it – I believe it's a bit raw at this time – I want you to come back.'

He wrote out some prescriptions and I left the office.

Nothing seemed to help. At home that night, I decided I would return to boxing to fill the days. The nights could be arranged with a fellowship and it was in my mind to join the Freemasons, just like my dad. And then there also was Geelong RSL.

I spoke to my kids a lot more. Joe suggested that I walk a lot and talk to God. Joe believes. God works in mysterious ways and maybe that's the way to beat the black dog.

I never returned to the shrink.

I invented my own recreations. Therapy was to be a lot more work in the garden and keeping the house clean. All those chores ought to help.

However, something from my past sticks in my dreams. A matter which I am not proud of and could have done better with: my celebrity friend, and client, Johnny Bean, who I dismissed one night and did not offer a room. The consequences of my actions may have been the reason for his death at the hands of others. How can I find a way around this to answer to the universe? Perhaps a synchronicity is just around the corner

3

The other player in this drama was Judy, my lover back then. We were travelling okay up to that night when Johnny banged on my door. She ducked into the bedroom, but she heard all the words between Johnny and me and left a note in the morning: 'We're going nowhere, Edgar. I'm not impressed with the way you handled Johnny.'

I still have the note. I have to find her.

I was walking the streets of Frankston, not far from the naval depot where I trained. I was not thinking about a connection as, after all, my naval career didn't involve Johnny. Joe says that we are all connected and I now believe it, due to the amazing things which come into play.

I walked into a bakery and surfed the menu, looking for a Cornish pasty. The female baker walked out. I gazed at her face and saw the big smile that I always loved about Judy. I was speechless but she wasn't. She darted around and hugged me. She put out a Gone to Lunch sign and the conversation started.

'I think about you a lot, Edgar. In fact, I dreamed about you a few nights ago. My, you have moved on in the book world.'

'I still have your note when I copped a spray about Johnny.'

'I blamed you but later on we found out it was going to happen anyway. Too many connections to the drug trade.'

'Still doesn't get me off the hook. Do you remember all that was said?'

'Vividly. I remember him gunning his car after and roaring off. I offered you a cup of tea. I didn't know that you were friends with famous musos. I knew later that you published his story. He was my hero. If I'd known the connection, it would have been a lot easier to get me into your bed.'

I smiled at her remark and she went on with her recall.

'How did you know him?'

'Primary school. Helped him with a lot of paperwork. He was always going to be a star. I heard that he had got into a sort of Mafia crowd and the rest is history.'

'What was he like?'

'Insecure. He wanted desperately to be your friend. He'd give me little presents – silly things which always made me laugh. I liked him very much. Too bad fame turned him into an asshole. I also remember you offered me that special tea but I wanted coffee. and you also had a shot at me about coffee keeping people awake. I didn't want to go to sleep that night. I felt rotten. I should have let him stay. What kind of person am I anyway to turn away an old friend who comes to me in the middle of the night pleading for help?'

'But you said it was just his imagination. That I also recall.'

I nodded but had to qualify my words again. 'Yeah, but what difference does that make? Imaginary problems are every bit as bad as real ones. Worse. Real ones you can deal with – you can call the cops. Imaginary problems you're stuck with. Jesus, so many years ago I wouldn't have treated him like that. Maybe this world of words has made me into a bastard. Maybe failure can louse you up just as badly as success.'

'Oh, Edgar, stop. You're not a failure. You're a successful publisher.'

'Even if that's true, I had to work my ass off to earn good dough. Judy, there's money out there and I see the Mercedes parked bumper to bumper outside the giant publishing companies. Still, I'm comfortable.'

'You once told me they were leased.'

'They are leased, but even leasing costs a bundle. That's the real reason I was rude to Johnny. I was eaten up with envy then. Years ago, we were on the bones of our arse, yet he became a millionaire.'

I ate my pasty.

Judy opened the door and leaned over. 'I forgive you,' she said and kissed me on the cheek. 'Get over it, Edgar. It was bound to happen.'

We shook hands and I drove away, tossing the piece of paper out into the wind and hoping for no more bad dreams about Johnny.

*

The older I get, the clarity of images from my youth explodes in my dreams and my walks. I was thirteen years of age and I read a lot, encouraged by my smart mother. What else was there to do? Dad worked long hours and in 1948 Australia was going in other directions. Dad and I still sparred on the lawn and I forget how many times I was flattened. But I always got up. I used to sell papers, which was encouraged by my parents.

I spotted an article in the newspapers which hung on the back of the outside toilet. My favourite article was by a Charles Atlas who promoted his course which guaranteed to make you a man 'in just seven days'. There were images of thin kids with pipe stick arms being bullied at a beach and drooling over the sixteen-inch muscly arms of the bully; the trophy gorgeous girl walking past, the thin kid, and kicking sand in his face. The kid was me in a dream every night.

The small book with instructions came to me in the post. I tore open the package – 'In just seven days I can make you a man.' After seven days of standing in front of the steamed window and using dynamic tension, which consisted of pushing against my hands, with a tape measure nearby to check, I expected a miracle. It didn't make a difference to the size of my arms. In fact, they were smaller. I purchased a set of expanders which did increase my biceps.

Charles made a lot of money from us suckers. I gave his program away and went into boxing, where there were free weights to use, chinning bars and lots of push-ups.

Charles kept on with his courses, with a litany of courses such as 'Increase your height' and 'How to get a ten-inch penis'. ('The girls will love you' was the postscript.)

I never sent away to find out more about those outlandish claims.
I did hear of a kid at school who tied a dumbbell at the end of his
member and as a result was treated at hospital. After a couple of
attempts, all he had come up with was a much longer version which
looked like an asparagus stalk.

*

Much later, Jackie and I gave in to nostalgia and went to see a rerun
of *The Rocky Horror Show* and in that strange but funny movie were
the old words from the days of my attempt to improve my body size.
'In just seven days.' We told the kids about it. They laughed when I
told them about the Gothic-looking kids all with black underwear and
make-up. They especially laughed when I told them my story about
trying dynamic tension.

4

Joe visited, on his bimonthly stay, with permission from his boss at the Melbourne Botanical Gardens. There were the usual questions like 'Are you coping? Are you getting out a bit? Are you talking to God on your walks?' They were answered in the affirmative. That said and done, he talked, as he liked to do, about stuff which he had read, and on which he put his own mark, writing comments in the margin.

The expression on his face said, 'It's comfortable, good coffee over there, let's go.'

The narrative started and I mused about what a kind man he turned out to be. I never interrupted any of his insightful words.

'We all have the potential for greatness, but it's ploughed out of us early. Fear enters when someone tells us there's a first prize, a second prize and a third prize, that some efforts deserve an A and some get C. After a time, part of us becomes afraid to even try. The only thing we have to give the world is our own grasp of it. The ego argues that's not enough. It leads us to cover up our simple truth, to try to create a better one. It's guarding against our experience of who we really are and the brilliance of expressing it.

'We really can't fake authenticity. We think we need to create ourselves, always doing a paste-up job on our personalities. We're trying to be special rather than real. We're pathetic in our efforts, trying to conform with all other people trying to do the same.

'Perhaps we should, at times, cast back to the honesty of children – like the story of a little girl who showed her teacher a painting of a tree. The tree was purple.

'The teacher says to the little girl, "Sweetheart, I've never seen a purple tree, now have I?"

'"Oh," says the little girl, "that's too bad."

'How's that, Dad? Out of the mouths of babes – not unlike the emperor's new clothes.'

I sat back and thought about Joe – my son the botanist. A tree hugger who had all the hallmarks of an activist regarding climate change and I silently applauded him.

He went on with another matter on his mind and asked for my opinion. 'Dad, do you think people need a PhD to get on in life, to get a great job? It seems our values are now based on our credentials – our resumés.'

This is one of my babies and I was pleased that he had broached the subject. 'Some of the best and brightest of any generations were educated more by life than school. There's a mass of talented people in our society who have been everywhere and done everything but have few credentials to show for it. Our achievements have been merely internal. I was once asked by a critic at a launch who knew that I promoted unknown writers from time to time. Some of them had a struggle with mainstream publishers and the critic wondered why I wasted my time on those unknown writers.'

'I know, Dad, about those intellectuals who won't have a bar of unknown writers.'

'I don't care to name them, though – as I'm still editing unknowns who don't have any letters of accreditation after their names. There was critic who remarked that authors should have to at least have undertaken the beginning of a university course before he'd think of viewing their work. He then asked if I knew of an artisan who had written a bestseller. I was quick in reply. "Winston Churchill – does that rate in your plimsoll line?" I gave him my death stare and he made an excuse to go to the toilet. You know me, son – still a bit of the violence left from boxing. I felt like smashing that critic. He left a full glass of single malt scotch and ice. So I drank it.'

Joe sat up and I watched the grin wash across his face, his lips ready to respond. But before that, he remarked, 'My dad the fighter – belts his way out of trouble.' He reached over the table and patted my hand. 'God doesn't require a resumé.'

I realised from that time that he would endeavour to transform me into a love-all fellow. But I was not ready to swing over to the good side 24/7. I'm happy with my walks and talks with the creator – that's enough for the time being.

*

I woke early after dreaming about critics. The office needed a clean – maybe a makeover – because it was neglected after the passing of Jackie, who did all the house cleaning. Joe's noisy snores told me he was sleeping peacefully, and as quietly as I could old I lobbed first drafts and out-of-date memos into boxes for a ride to the recycling depot. I scratched around muttering, 'Where is that piece? I want to read it to Joe before he drives back to the big smoke.' I had a flash of memory. It was Paul Hogan – he had something to say about critics around 1986. Then I saw it poking out from under a boring speech I once delivered. It was Hoges's video of his life. I've been a fan of Paul right from the start. I believed his talent was raw and original and he used the jargon of the man in the street.

A critic in the early days was unkind and wrote, 'I watch your performance with eyebrows arched in derision and my jaw cracking with boredom.' Another one wrote, 'To present Hogan as an original wit is a stretch of a flimsy talent altogether too much to embrace.' I smirked – well, he outlived you, you jerk.

Hoges by then had little time for critics, being full in accord with Cecil B. DeMille, who once said that he made pictures for people, not critics. About eighteen months after his venture into television Hoges said, 'The only publicity I ever got in the first year was bagging. I thought it was a bit rough. I didn't get hurt, just indignant. Being hurt is for big Sheilas. I've learned my lesson. I don't take any notice of those morons, don't ever bother to read them. The last time I read one, he said I wasn't a Bob Hope, for which I am very grateful. Who wants to be Bob Hope, standing in front of the cameras telling other people's jokes from a bit of paper. I don't mind being called rotten, boring, vulgar, ignorant, but I do mind those misinformed clots who say condescendingly, "And all he needs is a good scriptwriter. I'd love to have one if I could find a person who didn't take three weeks to write a three-minute sketch. Another prawn suggested I should have acting lessons. If I had acting lessons, I'd be in *Dad and Dave* [an old radio show] not me own show.'

Joe walked into the office with two cups of tea.

'Do you remember when Paul Hogan hit the scene, son?'

He could only nod, as he had a mouthful of the fluid.

'Read this. It answers your comment about talent. Hoges has a raw slice of it. And he's a millionaire by the way.'

'Thanks, Dad. I'll tuck this away for a rainy day. You're right about talent.' He waved and drove off.

The house was quiet again. So I thought.

A vehicle pulled up in the drive. It was Joe again.

'Forget something?' I said.

'Yep. Jillian's back – in Tassie.'

I was immediately happy that she was no longer in the war-torn countries doing her war correspondent stuff. 'What about the tragic Russian pianist?'

'Nup, too much vodka. She bailed out. Sh'es working out of Hobart with *National Geographic* as a writer. Her new man is one of the photo journos. I reckon he'll suit her just fine. She's very happy with him. They're hooked up with Greenpeace and she might be able to swing a trip for me down south to spot the whales, and the damage being done.'

'What does Lisa think about that?'

'She's also a secret activist but keeps a low profile. You should know about that, having once beena sailor.'

'Different then – though albatrosses and dugongs weren't touched so there were some bosses who were easy peasy about wildlife.'

'She'll ring you soon. Gotta rush, Dad. Keep me posted.'

And my depression eased due to the safety and the directions of some of my family.

5

I entered the sidewalk café on the way out after checking my bank balance. There was a familiar face at a table drinking coffee; he looked downcast and as I walked to the toilet I remembered him. I washed my hands and walked near his table and thrust out my hand, which he took, with a puzzled look on his face.

'I'm Edgar Williams. I was with my dad when Geelong won a prelim way back. We shouted along with all the old crowd. From memory, you were a Vietnam vet – you took us to your club after and Dad met a lot of old soldiers he knew. You were a siggy there and went back into that trade afterwards, right? You're Clarrie.'

'Bloody hell, Edgar, you were a subby on the *Sydney*, which took us there. I think you left the navy before that and I reckon you're a book publisher now.'

I nodded in response.

'God love his soul, I knew your Dad. He won a medal.'

'Yes, he did. Dad and Mum died a time back. And I'm still publishing.'

'Married?'

'Three times. Last one was the love of my life. She died. I still care for her.'

'Join the club. Two divorces since you and I met. Can't seem to get it right with the other sex. Get a coffee and sit down. I'm all ears, Edgar.'

I did as he suggested and returned with a short black with cream and sugar – have to keep the calcium going, as the quack says. I gave him my version of troubles in précis form, lest he nod off during my rambles. I started with Dad's funeral and went on about my sadness in losing them. He listened intently, without any interruption.

'So, Clarrie, what's your life like – not happy if I'm any judge of facial expressions.'

He swallowed his drink in one large gulp and asked the waitress for another of the same.

''My situation has gone beyond repair. The job went west after Jen decided she wanted to be a lesbian.' He stopped for a second – maybe for me to take in what he said.

I sat with my mouth open. My eyes were as large teacups and I reckon I looked like a meerkat. I took control of my racing thoughts. One came in which I couldn't stop: Joe always said, 'Look around, Dad. Messages come from everywhere like a source sent to inspire us.' And this was such a moment – just like he said.

I quickly recovered and added something appropriate. 'Well, this is new, mate.'

A tear ran down his face as if an internal conductor of an orchestra had pointed to the trombone player. 'I'm a basket case now. First the job then Jen goes in another life direction. No kids, thank God. The house went because, unknown to me, she borrowed money for the Devil's machines, as I call the pokies. And as no wages were coming in, the bank foreclosed on the mortgage. Precious things began to go one by one. Small pieces of our joint families, one old box after another to the thrift shops. My privacy started to close when the bailiffs searched the house. Our loved pets went to animal houses only to be killed one day later, which broke my heart. I would have killed her if only I'd had a gun. I remembered an old soldier who had a .303 stowed away. I planned it down to a T. My car went and I thought that was the end of it.' A dribble ran down Clarrie's face. He wiped his lips because the snot was on his chin.

I asked a question. 'Surely there's not more, mate.'

He cupped his hands around his chin. 'Try motor neuron disease.'

He stopped, staring in my face. It was like a comedy routine which should have had a happy ending but instead turned into a melodrama

'That's it, mate. The Vietnam vets are getting me a disabled veteran's home in two days' time. Sounds like that old joke about the soldier whose feet have been blown off and the bloke next to him says, "Hey, Bill, I have some good news for you." And the soldier with no legs raises himself up on his elbows, waiting with bated breath for the good news. "My mate wants to buy your slippers."'

I confess to bursting out in laughter. I was proud that Clarrie still had a sense of humour in spite of his impending death.

'So really, Edgar, what have you got to worry about?'

I ruminated on that and my situation, which was far from Clarrie's. I had to think of something to end the whole sad chapter in his life. I think it may have sounded hollow. 'Can I give you a lift anywhere?'

'The van's picking me up soon but thanks for listening. This is where I'll be.' He thrust out a card.

I was sure I would contact him. I chalked a note back at home, thinking I must do this – not like when I was too busy to help Johnny Bean.

6

I sauntered into the Geelong RSL after my boxing routine and a swim to brush off the sweat. I also had some blood on my forearm because my opponent hadn't had one of his gloves tied up. A couple of faces greeted me and I heard some remarks about my love of punching. I kept on strolling, itching for a pint of ale to quench my thirst. Some of Dad's mates were sprinkled in the crowd and they waved to me.

A tug on my sleeve caused me to turn round. It was Desmond Callie, who was a boy cadet who came on board the *Sydney* when I was being bullied by Black Bart, the commander. Desmond stayed for a time in the RAN and served on the *Hobart* in Vietnam. We met up after he was invalided out. He also knew my story and why I bailed out; after all, it was the talk of the ship. He also watched when I won the bout later on near the equator.

His face was as grey as a battleship. I sat with him and watched when he coughed consistently into his handkerchief. He took a swing from a bottle of Jack Daniels.

'How are you, Des?' It was a silly question as any observer would have guessed that he was on the wrong side of fifty and sliding.

'Not so good, Ed – copped a load of the dreaded asbestos.'

I was quiet for a few seconds, well knowing how many sailors had died with that disease as all the ships had their lagging full of the material. I tried to change the subject. 'I remember our last reunion some time back. Your wife was named Ruth, I recall. A chatty woman.'

He took another gulp of JD. 'Ed, I had a brain fag not long after that, with my hormones and a barmaid, with lots of sex, It caused me to make a fatal life change.'

I knew what was coming next.

'I knew I had to give Ruth up. I knew that moment when you can still walk away, free and clear, without lasting injustice on either side and just before that moment when somebody's going to get hurt.' There was a long coughing pause.

'Bad decision, Des, I imagine.'

'The very worst. The barmaid shot through. Six months later, Ruth met a wealthy businessman who took her to live in New Zealand – always someone waiting on the sideline from what I've heard.'

'So what have you been doing since the break-up, mate?'

'Got run over by a pushbike in the city.'

I suppressed a giggle.

He went on with the story. 'I had a visit to make to the shrink. Waited on the footpath for the Don't walk sign and till all the cars had passed and would you believe it one of those crazed messenger men on bikes slid through and pushed me back onto the footpath – result, broken ankle.'

'Shit' was all I could say.

'Fair dinkum, if it was raining fannies I'd get hit by an arsehole.'

We walked outside and gazed up at the stars and urinated on the prolific lemon tree, which was always in season.

'Heard your great missus had died, Ed.'

I looked away and shuffled my feet and felt the moisture that came into my eyes when people mentioned Jackie.

He guessed. 'Depression?'

I nodded. 'Supposed to be getting therapy – not much good for me. Best I keep boxing.'

'Don't tell me about it – just a lot of fuckers.' He reached for his wallet and pulled out a card.

I read it. It was the strange name of a local medium.

'I went to this woman – mainly to find my directions.'

'My son Joe believes in it. He's very spiritual. I'm open. So, okay, what did she say?'

'It's ongoing – things are happening. Look, if you go, don't be shocked at her appearance. She's Cajun, from Louisiana. You may need a couple of visits as well. Keep me posted. I'm here each Friday. See yah, Ed.' He waved goodbye.

*

I mused about it and finally decided to seek her out.

I knocked on the door of the old cottage. A squeaky door opened partially. A female voice swore and out rushed some cats. She stood and we stared at each other.

A hall light came on and she said, 'Come in. Mind the dog. I'm Maria.'

I sat on a comfortable chair and studied her. She was ancient with dark mottled skin. A humungous shawl with many patterns was wrapped around thin shoulders but her voice sounded a bit like a knife scraped on pewter. Her long white hair was carefully manicured as were her long fingernails. An azure blue cloth encompassed the great oak table.

'This is a crystal ball, as you can see.'

There now began a blinking contest and perhaps to break that steady silence she pulled out a very old clay pipe and lit it up. It balanced on her chin, which looked brittle and had errant hairs spaced along it. She blew smoke close to my face and I moved back a bit. Her hands waved in the air like she might be able to bring down departed spirits. Her old eyelids held in golden yellow eyes which reminded me of gold nuggets.

In the silence, thoughts circled me of what Des might say when we met again. Of his approval of her and the healing she obviously was transferring to him. He had said, 'Don't laugh, mate – she is really helping. She's dug right through my past and my mistakes. I now talk to God as much as possible and ask him a lot. Don't know how long I've got. She won't tell me, though.'

So I waited now, scarcely wanting to breathe as those arms circled in the air.

'Your parents are here.' She described them. It was accurate. She went though my school, the navy and my present career, and the loss of someone very close. Regrets – great loss – betrayal – a court case – intruders to be careful – a threat of gaol and the media all over me. Headlines in a paper. A talk with an interstate radio man. A child's marriage. Rescue work for old friends and possibly some volunteer work. She saw bookshelves and written books.

We shook hands and I paid Maria a small amount of money.

She grabbed my hand and said, 'The intruders may be people from the past. Stay alert. Someone is armed with a gun.'

I drove home and vowed to stay on alert.'

7

I went on a shopping spree in accordance with Joe's advice, as he thinks I am only getting takeaway and eating a lot more at the clubs. He's right to a degree but I also wanted to stock up the freezer – just like Jackie used to do – in case Jillian and her new man come to stay. From time to time, I chucked out a lot of use-by date food.

I was stocking up the basket at the local Coles supermarket when I smelt a pungent odour behind me. I turned about and saw a dishevelled man with lanky, dark, greasy hair. He shuffled as though his feet were sore and also carried stained sheets under his arms.

I watched his blinking eyes, which contained verdigris when he moved towards the exit sign. It was a hot day, yet he was sweating, which is said by the police to be suspicious. As he moved around the store, I watched when he slid tins of sardines into his deep pockets. Passers-by were avoiding him and the smell became stronger. He reached the checkout counter and pulled from his pocket a crumpled five-dollar note.

The assistant was rude and held her nose. 'That's not enough, 'she shouted.

I pulled out five dollars more from my wallet and, handing it to the assistant, at the same time had some words for her. 'You ought to improve your bedside manner.'

I followed the decadent man out the store. His face was vaguely familiar. He stumbled across the park and it was getting dark. I was still on his heels and I had to know who he was.

A woman with two kids in a pram hissed at him when he brushed past her. 'Watch it, slob.'

He was heading to a makeshift tent further along in the bush.

Two young cops emerged on the scene, studying the crumpled cover. The man stopped. They came towards him. He turned round and stared at me and in that instant I knew in a flash. I had met him years ago in the Vietnam vets club. Back then he was vibrant and an all-singing all-dancing entertainment man, wearing his army baseball cap and telling jokes. He was Gerry Graves.

I walked towards the cops, who spoke to me.

'Do you know this man?'

'Yes – Gerry Graves. I met him at a Vietnam get-together that friends invited me to. I wasn't a vet, just a former RAN man. But I'm good with faces.'

The cops looked at each other and the one with two stripes and military ribbons on his left chest spoke. 'Look, we'll take him back to the station and get him cleaned up. Can you come for him in a couple of hours?'

'Of course.' I turned to Gerry. 'You don't remember me, Gerry. It was a while ago when you entertained us at that club.'

He looked blank and then whispered, 'Edgar.'

*

When I went to the police station, he looked much better and he went with me to my car. I intended to take him home and give him some good food. When we were near, he just darted off and though I searched I found no trace of him.

I had a phone call a few days later from the cops.

'Mr Williams, Senior Constable Johns. About your friend – sadly he hanged himself yesterday in the bush.'

I thanked the cop and put down the phone then contacted the Vietnam vets club and told them about the whole scenario.

'Thanks, Edgar. I remember you. You're the publisher who published one of our guys' stories. Gerry's wife took off and he had a disabled son. He was fired from his job. The funeral will be next week. He was a Catholic but suicide doesn't gel with that religion. Just another sad episode among our vets.'

I hoped he would be buried with a blessing. Anyway, I attended his funeral and the undertakers did him well. There was the sobbing wife and his son. I heard she would get the gold card pension. I made no judgements about her. Shit happens.

I was at home that night thinking about Gerry when ding bloody dong. The medium said I would carry out some rescue work soon. I had to contact Des and tell him, and probably make a time to see her again.

*

I told Joe the lot about the medium and all the stuff that might happen; about the rescue – or the attempt to save another soul – and how it came to pass.

'I'm proud of you, Dad, as all of us are. You've always been a colourful person and no one expects you to turn into a Mother Teresa; But we do our best and you've helped a lot of people over the years without asking for praise. I'll send an email attachment which you might like.'

Here is what he wrote about love in the attachment.

'Love is within us. It cannot be destroyed, but can only be hidden. The world we knew as children is still buried within out minds. I once read a great book called *The Mists of Avalon*. The mists are an allusion to the tales of King Arthur. Avalon is a magical island hidden behind huge impenetrable mists. Unless the mists part, there is no way to navigate your way to the island. But unless you believe the island is there, the mists won't part.

'Avalon symbolises a world beyond the world we see with our physical eyes. It represents a miraculous sense of things, the enchanted realm we knew as children. Our childlike self is the deepest level of our being. It is who we really are and what is real does not go away. The truth does not stop being the truth just because we are not looking at it. Love merely becomes clouded over, or surrounded by mental mists.

'Avalon is the world we knew when we were still connected to our softness, our innocence, our spirit. It is actually the same world we see now, but informed by love, interpreted gently, with hope and faith and a sense of wonder. It is easily retrieved, because perception is a choice. The mists part he when we believe that Avalon is behind them.'

And that is my son Joe. Where he gets those words from I will never know. Maybe God inspires him. It seems so. I am aware of his thoughts about miracles and maybe it comes down to the parting of the mists, a shift in perception and a return to love.

8

I'm not as advanced on that ladder which Joe is climbing. I couldn't overtake him on his climb and I'm not ready to even twist around and climb up the other side. Yet I am talking a lot more to God. My thoughts are turning over like an empty carton being blow away by the wind, powerless with the power of nature but, with the years of editing, I can certainly keep up with the world of words.

At what stage, I pose, do we realise that we know the lyrics but not the music. It gives rise to ponder on that Undiscovered Country so frequently used in prose and attributed to Hamlet. That is when we may undergo a metamorphosis in our values. The concept we once held seems pointless when we exit from life to an unknown plane where no traveller returns. Yet it somehow excites me and always has, and on my Friday walk and chat with the maker I shout out, 'Okay, God. I've got a question to a puzzle about my life.'

He did not answer audibly but the wind did. I guess he controls the wind as well. A gust of wind blew off my hat. I chased it down the dusty footpath and found it under the shiny black shoes of an old detective who visited our place as a kid and who was one of my dad's corporals in the war. Dad wrote his autobiography as a rough draft and sent to his friend Mr Banks, who was a publisher. I was privy to the anecdotes I recall one of them. Mr Banks was not keen on autobiographies as he considered them to be unreliable. A lot of what is remembered is designed to shield the reader from the truth. The author easily forgets the words and what is to be kept or thrown away.

In one of the anecdotes which Dad and his cop mate shared, a fairy costume was ordered by the boss to help make a crook look like a fool in court. The crook always referred to the cops as fairies. He was about to be maggies' meat. On arrival at the cop shop, the crook was ushered into the locker room. A young cop dressed as a fairy, with a wand, sat on top of the locker. The crook kept staring at the fairy. The interview started and got nowhere. The crook pleaded not guilty and in his evidence said that a fairy was sitting on top of the locker and waving a wand. He told the judge, who naturally did not believe him and sent him up for several months. He never got over telling everyone that fairies sat on the top of lockers in the cop shop and finally ended up in the loony bin. Out of action and no more breaking and entering. Tough stuff.

I asked the old detective, who was still pinning my hat under his foot, if the story was true.

'Bloody oath. We had a priest outfit too, as well as a bear suit and a clown outfit. Great fun.'

To end the anecdotes I took him into a nearby pub and bought him a pint. I guess nowadays those detectives would be sent to gaol. Times have changed. I suspect in today's times, the crooks run the show.

9

The rear of the old house has a view of large open land. My parents fought the council for many years because they tried to use it for housing in spite of the fact that the land was donated years past to the council on the premise that the land be kept for future generations to enjoy. My parents won.

It still remains in the same state, with a gazebo, a dog park, a playground a cricket pitch, public toilets and a tennis court A creek runs right through the land along with gravel walking paths to the city Cyclists frequently use the tracks but motor vehicles are not permitted.

Dad created a fence with recesses all along which proved to be a godsend. A gate was put in, which was always used by the family to walk to the Freemasons club and the Geelong football club. I spotted a tent erected in the middle of the land and alongside was a motorcycle. It set bells ringing about Maria's words and I kept an eye on the tent.

My car was in for repairs and on a cool night I walked to the club. The house lights were on. On my way back, the lights were out and I saw a flickering torch in the office area. I was now on high alert because I also saw that the motorcycle with a sidecar was parked in a recess. I checked and under the lap rug were silver ornaments and some other material, plus two full-face helmets.

I crouched down nearby and then saw a man and a woman walk out towards the motorbike. I was close to them and yelled. The man turned round and pulled out a hand gun but before he had time to point it I hit him on the arm with my trusted old golf club. He tried again and this time the gun misfired and a bullet caught the woman on her leg. She ran off with blood spurting down her leg. He didn't have time to cock the weapon again. I hit him hard on his head and he fell into a heap – quite out to it. I rang the emergency people and they were soon there trying to revive the man. He was still prone and they loaded him in the ambulance and drove off with sirens blaring.

After making some notes, Tom, the old cop, who I knew well, said, 'It's Peter Bean – a lost druggie – and I guess the woman's his sister. They're the just-discovered kids of Johnny Bean, the famous muso dead all these years.'

I gasped with a realisation. Maria said there would be someone from the past. Poor Johnny. Now I might have killed his son was my thought.

Tom picked up the evidence and asked me to stay away for the night because of forensics, who had just arrived. To that end, I rang Mary and asked if she had a spare bed. While I waited for her to come for me, I checked the front door and saw that the lock was broken. I stepped inside and heard some muffled noises. I turned on the light and their was my great daughter Jillian – muffled with a gag. It appeared that she drove from Tasmania to surprise me – and what a surprise: she was caught in the drama. She was still shaking when Mary arrived.

I spoke to them both. 'Guess what. Tom tells me that the bloke I clobbered is Johnny Bean's missing son and the woman who ran off is the bloke's sister. Both druggies. What a world.'

We drove back to Mary's house. But all the way back I said to myself, Peter Bean, you stepped over the threshold. You have now inserted yourself without permission into my family and put my Jillian at risk. I don't really care if you're stuck in a coma for ever – don't try the victim on me.'

Jillian tried to talk things through. Pleasant things about James her mate, now on assignment on the Barrier Reef, but the shock came in, as did the tears, for which she kept saying sorry, all the time. Mary gave her a sleeping tablet and she was still out when I left to make a formal statement to Tom. Jillian would also have to catch up with Tom about her harrowing moments, not knowing if they would kill her as she memorised their faces. Joe was driving up on the weekend to catch up with all that had happened.

Meanwhile, unsure if I had killed him, I still laboured over Peter Bean. I am sure that somewhere in that misty world where Jackie exists they are able to direct stabs of forgiveness in our path, giving us unwanted choices which upset the apple cart and take us on another path.

It's all unfolding, Maria. How accurate you were with your reading. And now for the next stage of events. Anxiety outpaced all the other emotions. Which side would win? Positive or negative? After what happened to Jillian, some words which I had read fell into my chats with God: 'The thief shook himself free of his lies, like a dog rids his fleas of raindrops.'

10

I hadn't got a blue clue how the court system worked. I was put in the picture with Tom and the senior prosecutor.

Before that, I spoke to Tom about his opinions.

'Look, Ed, there are a few things you ought to know. There will be a direction hearing, after a bail application. It all depends on Bean's health. I believe he's still in a coma in hospital, so not much will happen till he gets better – if he gets better. If he doesn't, it might be a closed book.'

I sat there not wanting to butt in. Tom grinned at me when he pronounced about Bean and I guess the cops might be happy if another druggie gave them no more problems. If he was permanently rehabilitated, as they say.

'It looks as though the trial, if it's a trial, will be before Judge Murray – Murray Worry, but don't quote me outside of these walls. Pompous sort of fellow – that comes from being a QC for years. Loves crooks and worms around till he gets them a reduced sentence. Not madly keen on cops and, as you can imagine, he's in all the social groups. He's hoping to be nominated for the High Court, God help us. Once it comes down to the last appearance, I suggest you stay quiet till after the court. And knowing you it my be hard. You don't want to be like Derryn Hinch and get yourself a fourteen-day sentence for disrupting the court. Murray also hates the media. It isn't necessary for you to be there through all the hearing unless you want to be and it might also be a closed court anyway. That's about it, Ed. If you have anything to ask, feel free. How's Jillian coping?'

'Thanks for that, Tom. When will the prosecutor want to see me? With Jillian, it's hard to tell. She's a brave girl and she's lived in hot spots for some time.'

'Yes, I saw her on the telly a couple of times. We'll go over her statement with a fine-tooth comb. I don't know how we missed her from the start. Should have gone further in, which might be criticised along the line.'

'Have you heard about the sister – any sign of her at this stage?'

'Probably got fixed up by the mob doctor – a bit dangerous because their hygiene ain't good. A good chance if the bullet's not dug out that septicaemia could set in – and I guess she's already not in good shape. If he recovers, and there is a slight chance of that, I doubt that you'll have to give evidence as he'd probably plead guilty and I imagine his lawyer would plead a sad home life as is usual. In that case, he might be given, say, twelve months on the bottom with a suspended sentence and intervention with corrections and the wearing of a device on the ankle.'

'What if he partially recovers but with a considerable disability, say, paraplegia? Would he be in the dock or would it be heard by video – I've heard of that?'

'Usually there's a conference before that happens. At that point there'd be an army of psych reports, correctional reports, reports from social workers as to his life. Quite a bit of paper work, actually.'

'If he gets hard time in gaol, are there any consequences if he's in isolation 23/7.'

'There are many disabled people serving time with a background of crime before. A report would show the date of when he or she became disabled.'

Tom walked out with me. I expected that I might see him at the Freemasons down the track. I thanked him for all his help and promised to keep him in the loop of how we were coping. I professed to him that I wouldn't like the label of victim assigned to me.

Joe was at home having lunch with Mary and Jillian. He hugged me and spoke. 'How are you doing, Dad?'

Joe knows me and he would guess that I am a vengeful man when it comes to my family. I expected that he would hold his thoughts about the whole episode and not try to convince me to jump on the forgiveness trail.

I had the death stare on my face. 'Okay, I suppose, but it was a trying time and as the Duke of Wellington once said, "It was a damn close-run thing." You had to be there in those minutes to actually feel what it was like.'

'Yes. Jillian has told me how she felt – and she's been through harrowing moments overseas.'

'So what advice are you going to give me about this episode?'

'I saw from the start when you walked in with your lips held tight and the unblinking stare which I've seen a lot of in my life that it wasn't the time, date and place to offer my thoughts.'

'Come on, Joe, spit it out. Don't hold back.'

'So let's get this right. He tried to shoot you – fired off a shot which hit the woman with him in the leg and she ran off.'

'Right.'

'You belted him on the arm and he still tried to shoot till you belted him on the head with your golf club.'

'And do you think I did the right thing?'

'Who am I to judge – I don't walk around with a golf club hoping to hit someone.'

My hackles rose. 'So do you think that's what I do? Jesus Christ!'

'Settle down, Dad. You're twisting my words.'

'Bullshit – think again what you said. It was deliberate. I know where you're going with this – I did tell you to spit it out.'

'So where am I heading with this?'

'I think deep down you would just have caved in – preparing to absolve him for what you guess his life is like.'

'I'm not a coward, Dad. Of course I'd defend myself.'

'So if you had a brick or a hammer, what would you have done?'

'To save another, I would've used it. But you're missing the point, Dad.'

'What do you mean?'

'Look, you didn't know Jillian was tied up. You decided to act because they were stealing your silver and your Grange wine.'

'Partly right. I was angry but I didn't hit out till he threatened my life. Then I bobbed him on the scone. Stiff shit he's in a coma. At this point I don't care, Joe. You're really referring to my previous conviction when I hit that hoodie man in the same way. What are you? A defence lawyer?'

'This is going nowhere. Best I leave.' He started to the door and Mary chipped in.

'Your dad saved my life. That jerk had a great big knife.'

Jillian opened up. 'If Dad hadn't been there, I might be dead. Bloody get a life, Joe.'

He left the house and I vowed just to let it all die away – if possible. I didn't want another episode like I had with their mother Jane.

But I felt sad about it. They're adults now and I can't change them. Memories flooded back of how I let them stay with their controlling grandparents. For the best reason – as I thought – they would have a better life with all the opportunities that my in-laws could give them.

We always think that material stuff is best for kids – I did. Yet after this first ever duel in the trenches, the thoughts and the speech told me right then that they maybe missed them and that they also longed for their parents to be back together and hang the pool, the holidays, whatever they wanted, and the great Christmases.

Perhaps they had nursed the fact, with a bit of propaganda thrown in by the other side, that secretly they almost gave me up. At the end of the day, parenting is a tough job and one can't just disappear, and when it's convenient lob back and say, 'Hey, kids, come and live with me.'

*

I dreamed that night that a door was left ajar. To open it further was scary. It was full of intruders and robbers. A voice told me to search for key and that I needed a little openness because my heart was closed to any opposition. I had always thought of myself as an open person but it was a warning not to go much further until it was open for other people to see. So here I am almost like Joe preaching in the dream about the method to take for the heart to open.

In the dream, I was a secular person who wanted to be free of religion and all its problems. I had a challenge in life to create a sort of secular-spiritual type of religion. In that fashion, I might make Joe happy for me to fully turn to God.

I woke up and tried an autopsy on the dream but drew the conclusion that I was not ready for such a pivotal moment, a turn in my life.

One of us had to break the ice down the track. I had to forget my ideas whereby I try to get inside the right frontal lobe of my kids. Apart from boxing, which takes away the lonely moments, I might try yoga – or I might just join with some of those Spiritualist churches, mix with healers, learn their methods and listen to any messages coming in from the mediums. I hope with that I might be able to reach beyond the veil and talk to my beloved Jackie – if that can happen, then I am sold, if the evidence is accurate; and if it is, I will then sign up to be a spiritualist. Maybe write a book about it.

11

I am sat between two big detectives, listening to Judge Murray waffle on, which was largely about me rather that the perpetrator. I feel like the straight man in a knife-throwing act. Murray has quickly moved away from Peter Bean and constantly stares at me.

Okay, mate, keep it up. I reckon I am not bad at blinking contests and I think this overfed man with a face like an alley cat has never been in the human lions' cage, like I have, and came out on the other side, like I have. After all, I survived an obnoxious naval commander who had the power to keep me in the brig for a long time and ruin my career as well.

Murray drivels on about the poor man who is still in a coma and has been since the start of proceedings. The defendant at this point has never been in court. He is still in a secure hospital ward. Murray goes on about the gun and almost says that I caused the accomplice to received the wound by my action in knocking the gun down, which might have diverted the gun in another direction That offsider has disappeared and a warrant for her arrest is waiting for her capture. He is silent about my daughter Jillian tied up and muffled.

I have had enough and when a lull comes I stand and I yell. My hackles are up. 'So I'm the perpetrator and he's the victim, is that it?'

He just sort of ignores me and rustles papers and starts to read about me, mentioning that I have a previous penchant to belt people on the skull with a golf club, which sends them into a coma as well. I really have had enough of his pomposity.

Again I shout out words which just burst out from nowhere. 'You're just another fig jam, sitting on your throne.'

I quickly make myself scarce while Murray leans over and asks a clerk what 'fig jam' means. I'm gone.

I hear someone say, 'Stop that man.'

*

So here I am at home in my castle two weeks later while a great crowd has gathered with banners supporting me. And also a Sheriff Office car with two guys watching 24/7.

Mary and Jillian buy the food and I am looked after. The doors are locked and the sheriff people have given up knocking on the doors.

It's Mary who asks, 'What's this fig jam stuff? Forgive me for not being up with the local dialect.'

Jillian butts in – she has heard much in her life as a journo.

'It means "Fuck I'm Good – Just Ask Me".'

Mary chuckles and says, 'Murray must be a bit sensitive. So are you playing to stay. This is a bit like Derryn Hinch, I think.'

Jillian breaks in again. 'You know Dad – he'll stay with it to the end.'

I smile at Jillian's words but have to tell them my plans. 'Look, I'll walk out tomorrow, be cuffed and taken to court. He'll ask me to apologise. I'll respond with "You're kidding." I might say something that has a double meaning – like "I'm sorry I called you fig jam. I know better men than you who have that handle but they just laugh at it."'

'You might be there for a fair time – and James and I want you to give me away in Tassie, once we set a date.'

Another surprise – I'm yet to meet James.

'It looks like we'll have to marry in the gaol.'

I had spoken to Tom on the phone and he replied, 'Hey, you obstinate man – the buzz around is that it's an embarrassment to the government and the judiciary. Might take twenty-eight days but you'll be in protected custody – given a job to do, I imagine. When are you walking out then?'

'Tomorrow.'

'Will you say sorry?'

I confided in Tom what I would say.

I heard him breathing heavy but he said something else. 'The shock jocks in Sydney are onto it. Expect some words in your favour. They really hate piss-weak judges.'

'That's comforting.'

'You're gathering a lot of likes on Facebook.'

'I'll get Jillian to keep me posted,'

'You're sounding like a celebrity.'

'Not intended.'

'The guys at work reckon with all that's going on that the mainstream publishers will want to publish your bio.'

'That's stretching all of it a bit far, Tom, but thanks anyway. Not a great fan of some of those houses – they just want sensational stuff.'

'What do you reckon this is? The public love it. You've created a perfect storm, mate. If it goes bad, I'll do a few visits.

I tell the girls what was said.

'Are you sure you have no enemies in gaol? Like Murray was the one who kept letting them out.'

'Can't think of any except the daughter of Johnny who's still evading arrest – perhaps Johnny was generous with his cock.'

The conversation ends.

*

I walked out the front door at nine a.m. and was handcuffed and roughly shoved in the prison van. No beg your pardons – no conversation en route – no privileges.

*

I am in Murray's court. He walks in and the procedure I outlined to the family is played out.

'Get him out of here – now.'

I go silently into the van again and begin my twenty-eight days in cataloguing the library. It is better than the HMAS *Sydney* brig.

12

Judge Murray was finally given a package. I hope he does not return to the courts and double dip. God knows how much it cost the government but the heat came from many quarters of ordinary people who wanted real justice.

*

Joe congratulated me on the win but we never spoke again about our last moments of tension. He is on his path. I am on another. I am the green apple on the tree. He is the golden one.

The end of that drama left me a bit hollow. I was approached by a minister who had followed the whole dynamic from me locked in my castle, through to the courts and a return to handcuffs again. His view was bordering on what Murray said – so did I have another pillar of society judging me? I am unsure about some of those people who attend religious services and still maintain an air of superiority, of racial prejudices. Some take excessive profits. They encourage and promote a moralistic agenda and largely look down on people who have stuffed up – whether by design or accident. It's really not for me.

<h1 style="text-align:center">13</h1>

'Hi, Dad,' said Joe. 'Some news – good and not so good. Lisa had a fall on the ship and as a consequence she's on the way home. They've found her a hush-hush job in Canberra and I'm to move too to the gardens of the capital. The good news is you're going to become a grandad down the track. I'm excited on two fronts. I also have Lisa nagging me not to keep on about my spiritual ideas and I guess she's right because our family's expanding and I have more to think about. She's to be granted baby leave and we'll play it by ear. My guess is she'll stay at home after the baby's born, which would entail me working a short week at times. We'll wait and see. Jillian wants to be married in Geelong so you have some work to do. Just a clue – an idea…what about a big marquee in the parkland? I guess you could get permission from the council. And afterwards we could all walk over to the house and make a mess of it for you and Mary to clean up. Jillian's thinking a lot about our Mum Jane, who seems to have vanished into the ether, and she's on Google a lot. Maybe there's a relative of Jane who can answer the question. At times, I'd like know her whereabouts too. Gotta go, Dad.'

I now have another bit of work to do.

Jillian called – obviously she chatted with Joe about the wedding and her mother Jane.

'Yes, love. How are you?'

'Fine, Dad. Joe told me about his ideas for the wedding. Would that be okay?'

'Yes, love. Great idea.' I waited for her to say something about Jane. She did on cue. 'Do you remember Auntie Elsie in Mum's family?'

'Yes. A nice lady. Did you track her down?'

'I wanted to know about our genes and the breast cancer as Mum wasn't around when I was diagnosed. The medic naturally wanted to know.'

'Usual. So does Elsie know Jane's whereabouts?'

'Yes, she's in a private hospital in the outskirts of Melbourne. She suffered a bit from dementia and then you may have guessed – she has breast cancer, malignant. I'll go to see her soon. Not sure if she'll recognise me. Yes, you might ask am I upset. You bet, but I'm trying to cover it up.'

The old love which I felt for Jane long ago came into my solar plexus. I could feel a pain that spread up into my throat, which by now was tight. My eyes watered and I wasn't sure if it was due to the memories of the shock or the diagnosis.

'Are you okay, Dad? Your voice is cracking.' I grabbed a glass of water and gulped it down and said, rather weakly, 'Keep talking, love.'

'Look, Dad, I know that Mum was aloof and didn't tell us at any stage that she loved us. If and when I find her, I'd like to carefully tell her that I loved her and forgive her as well. If she's well enough, I'd like to invite her to the wedding. What do you think?'

'Do it if she can. I have no problems. I forgave her a long time ago and if I can I'll tell her so.'

'Right, Dad. As to forgiving, I believe there's no coming to consciousness without forgiving our parents. At a certain point, we forgive because we decide to forgive. We're not held back by the love we didn't receive in the past, but by the love we're not extending in the present.' She paused for a second with a sob and I heard her blow her nose.

'I'm back. There's a lot of talk about people growing up in a dysfunctional home. Who the hell didn't grow up in that world? The whole bloody world is dysfunctional and there's nothing we've been through, or seen or done, that can't be used to make our lives valuable now. We can grow from any experience and we can transcend experiences. Sounds a bit like the journo in me speaking, Dad.'

'And much like Joe's take on life. Keep me posted when you find your mum. Remember ,she lost both her parents as well in a crash.'

*

'I found her, Dad, just where Elsie said she was. I stood at the door not sure if I should walk in. I jumped on the bed, let out with a bucket of tears and kept on endlessly saying, "Sorry, sorry" to a blank stare. I walked out and spoke to the carer and wondered if it was at all worth it. The carer had another view and said, "There's a photo in the top drawer near her bed, of you, your brother and her. Sorry to tell you this: she hasn't got much time left, so the doctor says. Can you come back tomorrow just after she's had a bit of tea. She seems to be better after a meal." I promised I would. Dad, would you like to come as well?'

'Yes. I might wait in the waiting room, though.'

*

'Come, come quick. She knows me and wants to see you.'

I walked up to her but hesitated and then I heard a voice in my head, 'Go to her, Edgar. Touch her face and her hair for one last time.' And I knew then it was my Jackie speaking.

I obeyed and touched her face. That beauty with the high cheekbones and flashing white teeth smiled at me with recognition flooding her whole body when she sat up.

I hugged her and she whispered in my ear, 'Forgive me, Edgar.'

And out it came from my tonsils but in a muted voice. 'Please forgive me, Jane.'

I felt her arms slipping away down onto the bed. She gave a shuddering puff of breath and closed her eyes. The machine's one note played for a few minutes and stopped but Jillian sat holding her mother's limp hand when I walked out and waited in the car park.

*

The day is a cracker – brilliant sunny skies yet with a cool southerly keeping the flies away. A great day for a marriage. I engaged caterers from the club who worked in the house surrounded with its colour, the odours, hordes of gift cards and gifts. My stepkids sent apologies. Karen has an art exhibition. Jim has a grant for a mud-brick project in Aboriginal lands. They also sent money. There was marvellous prose written in longhand from people who could not make it.

I nearly tripped – Dad used to say I had two left feet. Wouldn't they have love to be here today. The gravel path also caused some discomfort for the bride but she soldiers on – straight back, satin dress and best of all a smile that would have bowled over a rough outback lad. She glows.

The band is in place – a naval band who offered a few weeks ago while I was at the club. They strike up a lively tune. Mary is advised to tell the caterers to rush in with the food if the weather changes.

My daughter on my arm – what more can a father have with his daughter? I confess to misty eyes. I hand her over to James, who stands straight in his dinner suit, as does Joe the best man.

I stand next to Tom, my cop friend, and a few of his mates. Not only do they honour me but the same for the wedding couple.

The female celebrant begins and speaks about marriage. 'Marriage, like everything else, can be used by either the ego or the holy spirit.'

Joe smiles at those words, which he might have used.

'Its contract is never predetermined. It is a living organism that enables the continuous choices of the individuals involved. Very little is sacred any more in this world, but one thing must be treated with reverence or else the moral fabric of the world disintegrates: an agreement between two people. An enlightened marriage is a commitment to participate in the process of mutual growth and forgiveness, sharing a common goal of service to God.'

And again Joe is happy with the words.

'The commitment of marriage is publicly declared when guests are present at a wedding to honour the rituals with blessed words.'

The celebrant concludes with all the well known words. Rings are exchanged, a book is signed and they kiss. We all clap.

Dancing is first with the band and the naval gal sings some modern songs from The Eagles, the Beatles and others. Food is consumed. The guests move around.

One asks me what it's like to spend twenty-eight days in the slammer.

'Met some fellows there who were extremely intelligent. Met a lot of druggies that I wouldn't want in my house. The guards were good, as was the food and the library. Not much else. It was an experience. I an now officially Prisoner Number X409.'

I know he's itching to ask a question which the media keep flogging.

'I heard from the shock jocks that you might be asked to write about your time in the slammer.'

'No, thanks. I've had enough of fame. However, if it was to happen, the royalties would be donated to Legacy.'

I tell Tom about Mr Nosey Parker.

He respond, 'I bet he tells the world.' Tom, now divorced, is on the hunt for any prospects. Looks like I might be going to another wedding, judging by the glances from one of the females in the band. Tom is a striking-looking man but he is looking after his three teenage kids, which might be a problem.

It does rain but the food is by now in the house – thanks to Mary,

The married couple sleep over in the house. I drive them to the airport for their honeymoon in Port Douglas.

Later at home all is quiet – like a herd of wildebeests has feasted and moved on, leaving only soggy hoof marks.

*

I had trouble sleeping after that great night and pulled out a DVD of *Crocodile Dundee* – Hoges being one of my favourite Australians. When the DVD had run its course, I remembered something he said about his own second wedding.

'We knew this priest who's a ripper bloke. He's the sort of priest you have to queue to get to hear his sermons, he's that popular. So we decided on a Sunday night to have a surprise party. About twenty turned up, a bit of grog, good food and a good time. Well, about eight-thirty or so, I yelled out for a bit of quiet and told them we were getting hitched – follow me into the lounge. Their jaws dropped. They nearly fell over their Fosters when they trooped in and saw the priest in his finery. It was a great night for us. There wasn't a dry eye in the room. It was a particular great night for my kids. It's not everyday, let's face it, when five kids gets to see their parents wedding.'

Hoges – what a champ. One of my favourites. Raw Australian talent who had to battle his way forward against the odds. Critics said he wouldn't make a dime. Now he owns some of the banks!

After all the celebrations were done, I decided to join the local Spiritualist church, as I promised myself after that voice in my ear when Jane died.

It's not like I thought it would be. Ordinary folk gathering to listen to mediums, some hand healing in a back room, and I saw no frauds. I spoke to the leader and told him about Jackie.

'It's common place once a loved one has passed over. Obviously there's a wait for the current to line up. Most messages are only about stuff you'd know. Nothing earth-shattering. Most of us are gathered here because we're disenchanted with mainstream religion. You say you're talking to God but it may just be Jackie. I have a small group – we meet on Tuesdays. Pop along and meet some of us.'

I am intrigued and will take it further.

*

I am sitting with several people in the group. These are not airy-fairy people. One is a former Brit marine who fought in the Falklands. A woman is a concert pianist. A young bloke with hair to his boots is a great guitar man who incidentally knows my stepdaughter, the artist, and also plays with a country and western band in Queensland. Another is a schoolteacher. All are intelligent people who want to discover the secrets of life and do not like the usual religions. They are right up my alley.

I had heard about séances and how it's Devil's work. This was not anywhere in that league. We had to breathe deep in the darkened room. No fingers on glasses.

A woman in a trance brought a voice in – not hers, though. 'I am Derek. I was killed in the Falklands. Jim tried to save me. But it was too late.'

The marine from the Falklands said, 'That's my mate.'

And on it went, with passed-over people clambering to be heard. The leader Julie asked if there was anyone recently killed in a crash, homing in about Jackie.

I won't ever forget this. It was Jackie and the smell of her lavender brushed my nostrils. 'Take care, Edgar. Look after your blood pressure. And forgiveness is to be experienced.'

I was hooked and I was also taught healing. I continued because I like the group and I am not drinking as much and, yes, the quack tested my blood pressure and I was immediately given a prescription. But I still choose to live in this life.

Julie told me that after the contact from across the line Jackie might have moved on to another life. Another bloody life! I want her to be there when I go over.

I went back to Maria – the group know her and all reckoned she was one of the best mediums around.

Ted the schoolteacher said, 'What about her clay pipe and whiskers?'

I nodded, and thought again, yes, these are ordinary humans who have banded together for a bit of research. Not devils as the Church would have us believe.

*

'You've had a lot of experience since we first met, Edgar. Has it widened your mind?'

'Most decidedly, Maria.'

'You went to gaol, like I said, after you clashed with the judge.'

'You were right of course.'

She waved her arms again and after a lot of breathing, 'You won't like it but you're heading for forgiving a person who wronged you.'

'Okay – how long?'

'Time is a man-made thing. Up there it's all past, present and the future. Up there I can't say.'

'Should I start reading some spiritual books?'

'Yes. Get Neale Donald Walsch's *Conversations with God*. It's all in there.'

'Didn't he make a movie about that?'

'Yes. It will, as they say, knock your socks off.'

I took along a bottle of rum for her as I smelt it on her. 'Got a bottle of rum for you Maria. Want a drink?'

She jumped up and after three small glasses I thought it was time to stop. I left the bottle with her.

She slurred when she said, Thank you.'

It occurred to me that everyone is on the piss – even mediums.

I bought Neal's book. It is amazing but two hundred years ago he would have been hanging from a tree. Two hundred before that, he would have suffered under the Church tormentors and been burnt to death. Neal's book talks about many taboos which humans have created – God certainly didn't. But it needs to be read three times at least, to let it grab the reader. Some of those nut jobs in the deep south of the USA would be after his scalp and it would be too dangerous to drive to those areas.

*

Mary is back at her unit, still the carer for her disabled husband, who has MS. She cares about everyone but can be tough if someone tries to tackle her, like the foolish Bart did some years ago.

'How are the blood pressure tablets going, Ed?' She always calls me Ed.

'Quack checked the pressure. It's dropped, which is good. While I have you, I read something about the heart. An amazing organ. Want to hear about it? Sit down. Might take a few minutes.'

'I'm all ears, Go ahead, Ed.'

'How often as writers do we think about the old term which we use as got a heart – rather than a mind – yet unless we have a serious health problem we just go willy nilly taking for granted our most important muscle. The heart beats daily and delivers oxygen to three hundred trillion cells. It beats one hundred thousand times and pumps two thousand gallons of blood each day.

'I'm not the only one who believes that it's also a spiritual pump which circulates love over many of our relationships. There are many heart surgeons who are up with research that's being done with volunteers assisting and fixing hearts without surgery. The scientists now speak about love as a healing organ.

'Bernie Siegel MD says that laughter relaxes all the muscles – including the heart – and the pulse rate and blood pressure temporarily dives. Other have found that muscle relaxation and anxiety cannot exist together and responds after a good laugh. It's been tried and tested. But can a rat laugh? Joking of course.'

*

It's Tuesday and I am at the healing and spirit class. A couple of older women wait in the backyard for the séance to end. I guess as old timers they have had all the relatives from the parallel world to speak with and probably know a hell of a lot about that world. To them it's old hat and all they want is a bit of relief from their aches and pains with a healer instead of listening to others about Uncle Henry who passed on from having a bout of sex with his young Asian wife, who didn't try to revive him. After all, there are more fish to fry in Australia with too many gullible old men. Sometimes the readings are just like that – just mundane stuff which over time gets boring.

'You're coming on with your healing, Edgar.'

I followed the instructions. First rub hands together and then hold arm out in front and feel when the palms tingle as the gap is closed. At that point in time, place hands over the infected parts of the sufferer and hold them there till they feel the warmth.

'Josie thinks you're the best healer here and the pain disappears when you place your hands on her knee.'

'It's nice to hear that I can help some.'

'I keep hearing, Edgar, that you're on the verge of helping out others in different locations as a volunteer. No healing but maybe reading some pages of a book, which should be up your alley, talking to them and handing out some cakes which we make. Are you in for it?'

I was stuck for words. Anyone in the armed services knows the old rule: don't volunteer.

She watched my eyes flick about. 'Yes, I know. My dearly beloved was in the army and he was loath to volunteer. I had to drag him to a home and wait till he chose someone to talk to. But reading to them wasn't on his radar.'

I had to respond. 'Let me think about it.'

I did think about it for six months and was still not keen. Something might have to happen to change my mind, Maybe a dream – maybe Jackie might bob up again.

14

Six months and more have gone and I am now in Canberra with Joe and Lisa. Lisa is now mother of a newly born baby girl with the name of Janet, which was her mother's name. Janet Senior is also here and it is the first time I have met her. She is as elegant and tall and has a fair skin and still blonde hair, which reveals their Scandinavian heritage.

I am able to hold my granddaughter in the week which I spend here but I'm not into changing nappies, which is a legacy from fathers who always said. 'That's woman's work.' Sometimes I think I have missed out on that touch which must lie within the DNA.

Joe is ecstatic and I reckon his whole personality may change – it always does with babies and especially with girls. Look out anyone who dares touch our daughters. That is the long-held theme of fathers with daughters.

A baptism is carried out and though Joe is not a Anglican he goes along with it. I can see him going along with a lot more now that he is a family plus one.

I have longed for years to visit the War Memorial and have a friend to go with. Janet has had that longing many times as well.

I found it strange, though, to be in the company with an adult female and quite an attractive one as well. It took two days to cover the whole memorial. I met the president and other dignitaries.

Janet is easy to talk to. I am sure Joe has filled in parts of my life for Janet and one day outside the great building she asked me how the court case came about and about my subsequent gaol time.

I didn't hold back and she tossed her head back and laughed. That toss so reminded me of Jackie, who had some of those traits. She was interested in my career and how it came to pass: she had never met a publisher. I left out some bits – certainly my revenge on Black Bart.

Overall, I enjoyed her company and learned that her widowhood was due to her husband, a tank man who was much older than her, being killed in an explosion in Iraq. She confided in me that he was a hard man to converse with – she loved him but found it hard going at times.

Time to drive home. I hugged all and asked them to visit when possible. I included Janet.

15

A flash of brilliance came into my head. I could start small with my own bit of help for the environment. The parkland has a lot of cans dropped on the grass in spite of the bins provided. I decided to be the unauthorised can picker-upper of the parkland. I bought a can crusher and some strong bags and it was my intention to patrol the land each day picking up the cans, crushing them and taking them to the recycle depot, who would give a portion to charity.

I dressed in my old painting clothes with a strong rope tied around the waste to stop my left foot from tripping over. I also had my old navy boots, not a bit worse for wear, and out I went across the parkland picking up the cans. In time I had a bag full. Sometimes I would stop and talk to Jackie while I ate my sandwich under a great red gum. I soon became well known to the strollers, who smiled at me. Talking to Jackie in the daytime was not on when people were about.

A lady with a pusher and a cute baby in pink stopped to give the child a drink. I said hello and she scowled at me and shouted back, 'Dero.' For the uninitiated, the correct version is 'derelict', referring to a homeless man. A tramp if you like, not unlike Paul Hogan's sketch of Perce the wino climbing out of a rubbish bin.

I was a bit miffed about that. Like do they want me to dress in morning suit?

I walked home when evening was closing in and saw Mary at the fence. She was laughing. 'Jesus Christ, Edgar, what are you doing? You look like a hobo. Jackie would hide her face if she was alive.'

'Just doing a good thing for the environment.' I showed her the cans.

She was still giggling. 'Haven't you got some trackies to wear?'

'Not you too. Even a young mum called me a dero when I got near her child.'

'Not surprised, Ed. Promise me you'll at least put on some overalls.'

I had to comply and next day I did but I wore my old navy boots. There I was busily engaged concentrating on the task when I heard some teenagers behind. I turned round and they looked menacing.

The tallest one, about sixteen, was the leader of the pack and he moved in close yelling, 'Dero, dero.'

I backed up against a large tree trunk – always make sure your back is hidden when in trouble. The leader pushed me in the midriff. I diverted his fist and grabbed it and then twisted it. I threw him onto the ground and his other yellow mates quickly darted away. He threw a punch at me. I blocked it and hit him full on the jaw and down he went in heap. He rubbed his jaw and looked puzzled and I imagine his ego was shattered after tangling with an elderly man and being knocked down. I put out my hand and pulled him to his feet.

'I'm going to report you to the police.'

I laughed. 'I know most of them. They'll laugh you out of the station.'

Typical of the youth today – hate the cops but when someone betters them they want to rush in a make a claim.

'So why aren't you at school anyway?'

'My mum's left and she threw out all my books.'

I thought for a while about this kid and it sounded like he had a bad deal at home. 'Look, I train at a boxing gym. If you like to come, I'll teach you how to defend yourself. Let's walk. It's not far.'

On the way Alex told me his whole life story.

'What if I go to see the headmaster and get you some more books?'

Alex didn't know what to say. I had to tell him I wasn't one of those perverts who hang around parklands. He grinned at that – a grin of relief.

Alex spoke about what he wanted to do in life. He wanted to join the army.

'Tell me, Alex, are you on drugs?'

'I hate drugs. My older brother's in rehab.'

'That's a good start.'

We walked into the boxing club and I introduced him to the coach, who had a penchant for helping kids. I left him with Ralph. Before leaving, I gave him some money to buy a hamburger,

'Meet me at the school prompt. Eight a.m. I'll go in and talk to the head and a social worker.'

Alex was there cleaned up, as I was – not in my derro clothes. I introduced myself and explained the situation about his home conditions.

The social worker came in and spoke. 'Leave him with us, Edgar. We'll outfit him and find out more about his home life.'

I am proud to say that Alex is coming along fine. I talk to him at the gym and we spar. He helps his dad clean up the place. His father knew he had to shoulder the burden of both parents, and I called in to see him at times.

This is the sort of volunteering that pleases me. That I was able to pull a kid up from the direction he was heading.

I organised a large skip to take away a lot of rubbish – at my expense. Can't take the money with us when we pass on. I dumped the dero clothes in thet skip as well and Alex laughed when he said to his dad that I was helping with the loading.

'They're the clothes Edgar was wearing when we harassed him.'

I was thrilled about his words ,which were a step into understanding how other people react when threatened. It was a great lesson in his life.

A pivotal moment, I suggest. I intend to help his dad Max as much as possible with the best help I can offer – which is being there as much as possible. This is a project which is grass roots. Not getting some kid a great prize for having the best essay in the school, which at times causes grief when high expectations are not met.

<h1 style="text-align: center;">16</h1>

I never expected to cross paths with Peter Bean after I rolled him onto the three-quarter prone position with his right arm splayed out and the left arm draped over with the elbow at a crook. There I was trying to stop the blood flowing from his skull, which I skilfully belted seconds before. The ambulance people took over and as he was consigned to a hospital it was pointless visiting him.

And there I was with some of my spirit church people sashaying around, patting people on the back, pulling on or pulling off socks and wiping cream off the lips of people who really enjoyed their dessert. Some said thank you while most sat staring into space like a farmer waiting for rain or watching a kettle boil. I can't blame anyone but myself for this chore, which is supposed to create happiness in most of the inmates. I guess I think about me when I am very old and wonder if I might become another Gandhi loving everyone and getting shot in the process.

At times, I think of this life and the hints from afar and wonder if Jackie is really the urger. On occasions, she does seem to make herself present. For example, I was at the photocopier one day near the office at home: the window was open and there was a breeze blowing, and our album was near the machine. Inside were the pictures of Jackie and me in Tasmania, in the library at Hobart. I wasn't really thinking about anything else, except watching the copied sheets as they fell out onto the floor. I turned round and the wind blew over to the next page, with Jackie sliding down a slippery dip. It happened again – twice this time. I felt her presence. I smelt her perfume, Some people see butterflies, others clouds. Well, it was the wind for me and my dear wife trying to get through for some reason. A reason of high importance, I thought, and it must be something from the past as Maria had almost given me the précis of my future.

One night, I swear someone touched me. I'd sort of being asleep on the chair in the lounge room and someone touched me on the hand. I always thought it was her. It was a long time ago – about a month after she was killed. Somehow it was comforting and I wondered if she had suffered in pain. Jackie is definitely about the place.

A week later, we were booked to help a carer in a sort of a hospital with a lock-down security door. We all had to sign in and write in the time. I passed through many rooms, listening to crazed chatter, getting out of the way when patients ran along the corridors chatting to themselves. An old lady ran up to me and hugged so tight I felt her fingernail digging into my spine. I prised her head from my shoulders and she stared at me with a maniacal eye.

'How do you like that now, Fred – no fun, is it.'

The carers came along and freed her and she was still calling out to Fred when she was dragged off. I gained the impression that Fred was a bit of a tyrant.

We moved on and rounded a corner and saw a man in a mobile chair. His head was braced and I saw that his legs had withered. His head was shaven and the marks of surgical scars criss-crossed his head like a dragon pattern on a tattoo. A nurse had her both hands on his thighs and was talking quietly to the disabled man. I stood by the door.

'Come in,' she said. 'Are you one of the volunteers?'

'Yes. Just learning. How is this fellow doing?'

'He copes but we're not sure if he knows where he is.'

'How long has he been here?'

'Some time now. He was in a coma for years. I'm here part-time and he seems to know me.'

'What's his name?'

'Peter Bean.'

I swayed a little and held my head in the realisation that I had put him in this state – virtually a dead man in a chair. I clutched the edge of the door and breathed deeply.

The nurse stared at me. 'Are you all right?'

I mustered up some courage and spoke. 'He's someone from my past. I didn't recognise him.'

'That's normal. Most people react the same when confronted by this spectacle.'

I went outside and sat on a chair, not having the courage to tell her I was the one who put him in that state. A tear coursed down my cheek. Was this a dream of reality or was it reality which was the dream? My old ideas of vengeance began to crumble. I had to get out of there. I caught a taxi home and lay on the bed. Didn't talk to God or Jackie. It's my problem. How do I make amends or at least some atonement? Peter Bean would not recognise me or even what part he played in that drama.

I rang up Tom the practical cop – most cops are amateur psychs, – and told him what I saw.

'Wait home. I'll be around. I also have a friend with me.'

When he knocked on the door, he walked in hand in hand with the naval band gal and introduced her. 'The way I see it, Ed, is there's nothing you can do. If he was revived, he'd hate you, which you'd feel. You tell me he's a basket case. You won't get through to him.' He thought for a while and then had a suggestion. 'His dad was a brilliant muso with all instruments especially the guitar. Maybe that gene is in his son. Why not buy him a guitar and let him touch the strings. You never know. But for Christ's sake don't tell him who you are.'

I thought on this and it was a good idea. We spoke for a while about other matters. Patricia and he have found a love – in the formative stages. She has a grown-up daughter and his boys are looking forward to Pat teaching them music. Seems okay. I wish them the best.

I wandered around and found a nice guitar and took it straight to Peter Bean's room and left it with his nurse – with my phone number.

Later, the nurse rang me. 'Somewhere within his cells he knows how to play the guitar – you ought to come and hear him. The doctors are amazed. Thank you for your kind gift.'

I bet if she knew who had put him in that chair, she wouldn't be full of praise.

*

Six months later, I attended the home and they wheeled him in to a captive audience. I sat through the tunes he played. He will get better with his music but I shot through. I was also aware that his sister might have heard about her brother and turned up. I didn't want anyone in that crowd to recognise me.

I rang Joe and told him what I did and that just before the visit the incident kept coming back and hung on me. I was like a man in a cave who is lost and finds no exit, except when a rock dislodges and there is a passageway.

This is what he said. 'Our needs are not separate. If we contribute to another person's pain, it will always come back to haunt us. If we do what we can to help them, someone will always come around to do the same for us. It's not enough to sit idly by while others hurt, using the catch words like "Not my problem" or "It would be codependent of me to get involved" as an excuse for a selfish stance. A person once said to me after a situation in which I felt betrayed, "I never wished to hurt you." I said, "Love isn't neutral. It takes a stand. It's commitment to the attainment of the condition of peace for all involved in that situation."

Once again Joe came up trumps.

*

Jackie is here again. She is learning strange things which are a power bestowed on her. She can magically bring on an orchestra which wipes out the silly commercial jingles on the TV. If my car won't start, just ask Jackie and, whoosh, it starts. Cold water becomes hot water and vice a versa. She can't raise the dead, though. She also sits with me when the Geelong Cats play and she cheers with me. I hope that she doesn't watch when I'm in the toilet. That personal stuff is just that. She used to hate it if I burst into the bathroom when she was drying her toes. She concentrates on putting her image on the bevelled edge of the mirror, which must he hard. All of this stuff she explains off with words, saying that it's all down to energy and God is just that energy.

I tossed a curved ball at her after one of the bathroom bevelled mirror images. I wiped the shaving cream off and stared in the mirror. 'As much as I loved you, Jackie, and still do, is it possible for a man to love two women?'

I thought I heard her say in a wispy voice, 'What are you driving at, Edgar Williams?'

I have struck a chord here with the ghost because when she gets her hackles up it's always my full name.

I spell out one word. 'Janet.'

The silence is so tangible it could crack the overhead whirring fan.

She never answered that query yet I always believed that jealousy, and other like emotions, doesn't exist in the parallel world. I still have not found the answer, in spite of all the mind, body and spirit books which I buy and read – and later give away, because the spirit mates always say, 'When a book is read, pass it on. In that way, you're doing God's work in a small way. '

After that episode, I dropped off on the lounge and a dream of lights of many colours and depth kept flashing by which was like a lighthouse beam being directed over 360 degrees on each gyration and I experienced a healing wave into my stiff neck and wondered who sent it. Was it God, angels or just that little man inside of my brain who ticks away 24/7?

17

I see Janet when she drives down every second weekend of the month. We are great companions. I haven't heard from Jackie since, and my spirit friends think she has moved on. I miss those conversations and wonder if we will meet when it's my time. What will God say about me?

Maybe he will ask the archangel Gabriel, 'So who have we got on the list today?'

Gabriel will slide his finger down and say, 'Here's an interesting fellow.'

'What's his name?' God will ask.

Gabriel will giggle, 'Fig jam!'